Conamara Blues

JOHN O'DONOHUE

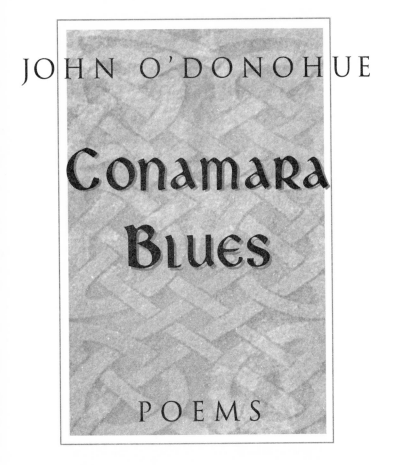

Conamara
Blues

POEMS

Cliff Street Books

An Imprint of HarperCollins*Publishers*

The author wishes to acknowledge the following publications in which earlier versions of some of these poems appeared: *Lapis, The Connacht Tribune, The Whoseday Book, Ireland of the Welcomes,* and *Departures.*

CONAMARA BLUES. Copyright © 2001 by John O'Donohue. All rights reserved. Printed in the United States of America. No part of this book may be used or reproduced in any manner whatsoever without written permission except in the case of brief quotations embodied in critical articles and reviews. For information, address HarperCollins Publishers Inc., 10 East 53rd Street, New York, NY 10022.

HarperCollins books may be purchased for educational, business, or sales promotional use. For information please write: Special Markets Department, HarperCollins Publishers Inc., 10 East 53rd Street, New York, NY 10022.

FIRST EDITION

Designed by Mary Austin Speaker

Printed on acid-free paper

Library of Congress Cataloging-in-Publication Data
O'Donohue, John, 1956–
  Conamara blues / John O'Donohue
    p.   cm.
  ISBN 0-06-019644-0
    1. Connemara (Ireland)—Poetry. 2. Christian poetry, English—
    Irish authors. I. Title.
PR6065.D574 C66 2000
821'.914—dc21   00–047487

01 02 03 04 05 ❖/QM 10 9 8 7 6 5 4 3 2 1

IN MEMORY OF MY AUNT,

Mary O' Donohue
(1896–1923)
of Caherbeanna, who died
in a tragic road accident shortly
after her emigration to America

CONTENTS

APPROACHINGS

ENCOUNTERS:
THE ROSARY SONNETS

The Joyful Mysteries   36

The Sorrowful Mysteries   41

DISTANCES

A P P R O A C H I N G S

I want to watch watching arrive.
I want to watch arrivances.
—HÉLÈNE CIXOUS

I think back gladly on the future.
—HANS MAGNUS ENZENSBENGER

Think of things that disappear.

Think of what you love best,
What brings tears to your eyes.

Something that said *adios* to you
Before you knew what it meant
Or how long it was for.
—NAOMI SHIHAB NYE

THOUGHT-WORK

In memory of Joe Pilkington

Off course from the frail music sought by words
And the path that always claims the journey,
In the pursuit of a more oblique rhythm,
Creating mostly its own geography,
The mind is an old crow
Who knows only to gather dead twigs,
Then take them back to the vacancy
Between the branches of the parent tree
And entwine them around the emptiness
With silence and unfailing patience
Until what was fallen, withered and lost
Is now set to fill with dreams as a nest.

FIRST WORDS

For Shane O'Donohue

Parents know not what they do
When they coax those first words
Out of you, start a trickle
Of saying that will not cease.
Long after they no longer hear
Your talk, the words they started
Continue to call out for someone
To come near enough to hear
The cadence of what has happened
Deep in the inevitable growing
Heavy and weary of heart
Under the layer of days
Where memory works cold fusions,
As if your voice could carry you
Out of the stillness to the warmth

Of someone who would linger with you
To search the frozen parts for tears
Until a forgotten line fires
Down through the word-hoard
To where your first silence was
Broken, and your rhythm born.

NEST

For J.

I awaken

To find your head
Loaded with sleep,
Branching my chest.

Feel the streams
Of your breathing
Dream through my heart.

From the new day,
Light glimpses
The nape of your neck.

Tender is the weight
Of your sleeping thought

And all the worlds
That will come back

When you raise your head
And look.

BLACK MUSIC IN CONAMARA

For John Barry

To travel through the trough
Of this Sunday afternoon,
As mist thickens into a screen
All over Conamara,
Holding the mountains back
From the clarity their stern solitude
Strives after, releasing the spring
Lustre of the long grass, ever further
Into a fervence of indigo, so much
So that the granite rocks strewn about
Seem eventually abstract, afterthoughts
To something that took place before them.

Take the silver bucket
Full of coarse turf cut from under here;

Light its brown shape in the grate
Until it blooms into a red well.
Put on a disc of smooth steel
That slowly builds, yields up a pulse
Of jazz from Roland Kirk,
Who never was here, but somehow
Played a live concert once, so full
Of the withheld litany
Of this shy, Conamara day.
The saxaphone catches onto
Some riff of murmur,
Deep beneath the roots of the mountains,
Where granite relents, giving way
In tears, to the blanket poultice of the bog.

THE WOUND AT THE SIDE OF THE HOUSE

For Pat O' Brien

The glistening, neon dome
Turned the night bathroom,
With its window open,
Into an addictive sanctuary
Which had drawn in
The masses of the night.
Thousands of demented ephemerae,
Needle specks of shivering flies,
Moths and myriad winged things
Congregate around its merciless,
Unrelenting light.

Having waited all day for the daylight
And its vestal colours to leave,

They arose from the bog,
Navigating rushes, grasses and briars.
Rising into the wonder
Of this night, with its moon
Casting mint light from behind
The mountains of Conamara.

On the adventure
Of their few hours of life here,
They had the misfortune
To pass by on this side of the house
And become at once entranced
By this strange window of light,
A white wound in the night,
Its drawbridge down,
And flew in to the blind worship
Of its deadly brightness.

BEFORE THE BEGINNING

Unknown to us, there are moments
When crevices we cannot see open
For time to come alive with beginning.

As in autumn a field of corn knows
When enough green has been inhaled
From the clay and under the skill
Of an artist breeze becomes gold in a day,

When the ocean still as a mirror
Of a sudden takes a sinister curve
To rise in a mountain of wave
That would swallow a village.

How to a flock of starlings
Scattered, at work on grass,
From somewhere, a signal comes

And suddenly as one, they describe
A geometric shape in the air.

When the audience becomes still
And the soprano lets the silence deepen,
In that slowed holding, the whole aria
Hovers nearer, then alights
On the wings of breath
Poised to soar into song.

These inklings were first prescribed
The morning we met in Westport
And I was left with such sweet time
Wondering if between us something
Was deciding to begin or not.

THE BANSHEE'S* GROTTO

After a photograph by Fergus Bourke

The . . . bean sí is a solitary being . . .
—PATRICIA LYSAGHT

I heard her across the river crying; a neighbour was dying.
—PADDY O'DONOHUE

The tear is the anticipation of the eye's future.
—JOSEPH BRODSKY

The messenger comes from that distant place
Beside us where we cannot remember
How unlikely it is that we are here,
Keepers of interiors not our own,
Strangers in whom dawn and twilight are one.

---

*The bean sí is the death messenger in the Irish folk tradition.

When the black door opens, she often appears,
Keeping her distance from the house of grief,
Circling it with her cry until her tears
Have cut a path to the nerve of a name
That soon will stand alone on a headstone.

No one has seen her face or can fathom
Why she comes so far to mourn a stranger.
She is no Rachel weeping for her children,
No Cassandra doomed to remain unheard,
She is the first voice from the other world.

It seems the camera's eye caught her form
Hunched inside a waterfall in Mweelrea.
Is it there she collects tears of delight
Sure that death is bright, or worn down with grief
Must she drink from her Conamara Lethe?

WIND ARTIST

For Ellen Wingard

Among the kingdom of the winds,
Perhaps, there is one of elegant mind
Who has no need to intrude
On the solitude of single things.

A wind at ease with the depth
Of its own emptiness, who knows
How it was in the beginning,
Before the silence became unbearable
And space rippled to dream things.

A wind who feels how an object strains
To be here, holding its darkness tight
Against the sever of air, ever eager

To enter, and with a swell of light
Dissolve the form in its breathing.

A wind from before memory
Whose patience will see things become
Passionate dust whorled into sighs
Of ghost-song on its wings.

ELEMENTAL

Is the word the work
Of someone who tills the blue field,
Unearths its dark plenitude
For the tight seed to release its thought
Into the ferment of clay,
Searching to earth the light
And come to voice in a word of grain
That can sing free in the breeze,
Bathe in the yellow well of the sun,
Avoid the attack of the bird,
And endure the red cell of the oven
Until memory leavens in the gift of bread?

THE PLEADING

All night long, and all through the white day,
The beat of the wind's bulk against the house,
Pausing only for a breath, and then, again,
The rise and wail of its keening, as if I
Could come out into it, and answer
Its unbearable grief with some sweet name,
From which it could make an antiphon
To calm down its demented legion
Of breezes, or failing that, could I find
And release a granite rock, to open
A duct in the mountain, for it to enter
And search the underworld for itself.

THE SECRET OF THERENESS

For Martin Downey

And the earth fled to the lowest place.*
And the mystery of the breeze,
Arising from nowhere, could be
A return of unrequited memory
Awake at last to a sense of loss,

Stirring up the presences in these fields,
Clutches of thistle roll their purple eyes,
Grasses wave in a trembling whisper,
Profusions of leaf dance slowly

On the low spires of rowan trees;
In fields and walls the granite ones

---

*Meister Eckhart

Never waver from stillness, stones
Who know a life without desire,

Each dwells in its own distance
From night acclaimed by twilight
And day released through dawn.

Utterly focused in their stance,
Stones praise the silence of time.

BREAKAGE

Life sentence. First night.
Whistles from cages in Hades.

♦

Black dog. He breathes for me.
Nowhere. Dead air.

♦

Months later. All normal.
Then, it hit her.

♦

Found letters. Too late.
The shock of who she was.

♦

Labour pains. Relief.
Then, the child. Damaged.

INNER CIRCLE

For John Moriarty

Stranger sometimes than the yellow crotchet
Of glimpses that civilize the dark, or the
Shelter of voices who stall the dead
Silence that longs to return to stone,
Stranger is the heart, a different scripture,
Weighed down by thoughts of gods
Who will never emerge, to recommend
One way above another to anywhere,
Lest they distract from the festival
Of vivid presence, where journeys are not
Stretched over distance, and time
Is beyond the fatality of before and
After, and elsewhere and otherwise
Do not intrude on day or night.

FLUENT

I would love to live
Like a river flows,
Carried by the surprise
Of its own unfolding.

THE STILLNESS ABOVE IS LISTENING

Rooted in the quiet earth beneath
Which enjoys the quiver as harebells

Relinquish perfect scoops of breeze
Absorbs the syllables when rain lowers

Its silver chorus to coalesce
With granite rocks terse with thirst

And tight with the force of unfreed voice
Feels the moon on its fields brightening

The length of night out into the nowhere
That would love a name like Conamara

The mountain remains a temple of listening
Over years its contours concede to the lonesome

Voices brittle with the threat of what is gathering
Towards their definite houses below

Harvesting the fragments of sound
Into its weight of stillness.

MOUNTAIN CHRISTENING

For Nöel Hanlon

Poor wounded name! my bosom, as a bed shall lodge thee . . .
—SHAKESPEARE

After a hard climb
Through a dry river-bed,
Its scoured stones glistening
Like a white chain to the horizon,
Descending between its links
The long concerto of a stream
Where the listening mountains incline,
Rising against the steep fall of soft bog,
Searching for our grip
In the shimmer of scree.
At last on the summit
Of the Beanna Beola,

Overlooking three valleys,
Delighted to be so high
Above the lives where we dwell,
Together for a while
From other sides of the world,
Sensing each other,
Strangely close,
Suddenly, your voice
Calling out my name.
I call yours.
The echoes take us
To the heart of the mountains.
When the silence closes,
You say: Now that they
Have called our names back
The mountains can
Never forget us.

THE NIGHT UNDERNEATH

Night carries blame for dream and
The other worlds, you become
Mother opening the door to
Walk inside the colour blue
Where animals wear haloes.

Frescoes that evaporate
Into the grey wall of dawn.
You waken to continue on.
Shake yourself free from the night,
Continue with yesterday's life.

Under the day's white surface
All the scripture has withered.
No word, no sound to be heard
In the long wind that reaps dust
From all the harvest of voice.

And the mind behind it all
Has dried up, left nothing but
Its ghost imprint active still
Listening to your footsteps fall,
Their music of red shadows,

Knowing that sooner or later
Some distant light will flicker,
Your blind feet will stumble on
That frail place to send your weight
Through the depth of paper earth.

DECORUM

In the winter night
By the lake edge
A stern breeze makes
The young novices
Of reed bend
Low and bow
To the mystery
Of a shadow-mountain,
Gathered the moment
The cloud freed the moon.

IMAGINED ORIGINS

For M.

Nothing between us, so near
I hear your skin whisper
What you could never tell
Of the longing that called us.

How through the branches
On to the clay beneath the oak,
A lace of light came down
To wait and watch each day,

And the secrecy of the breeze,
Dying down over the shiver
In the earth, hovering there
To blend its voice to breath,

How, even then, the rain
Through the brow of grasses
Could foreshadow tears
And the trickle of water change,

Or the fright of crows from trees
At dusk into the empty paleness,
This rush of black words today
Searching for you on the white page.

E N C O U N T E R S

THE ROSARY SONNETS

For Noel Dermot O'Donoghue

and in memory of Pete and Paddy O'Donohue

ὁ Λόγος σάρξ 'εγένετο
—Jn 1:14.

Love, like fire, can only reveal its brightness
On the failure and beauty of burnt wood.
—Philippe Jaccottet

To stand in the shadow
of the scar up in the air.
—Paul Celan

AN PAIDRÍN

I gcuimhne ar Cyril Ó Céirín

Ar nós cheoil na farraige
Tagtha sa bhfoscadh
Ar an teallach

Ag brionglóidí uirthi féin,
An bhrionglóid chéanna
Ó i bhfad i gcéin

Ag snámh go séimh
Idir thrá agus tuile
Na Sé do bheatha, a Mhuire.

THE ROSARY

As though the music of the ocean
Had come to shelter
On the home hearth

Dreaming of itself
In the selfsame dream
From a far distant region

In buoyant ease
Between the fill and fall
Of waves of Hail Marys.

The Joyful Mysteries

THE ANNUNCIATION

Cast from afar before the stones were born
And rain had rinsed the darkness for colour,
The words have waited for the hunger in her
To become the silence where they could form.

The day's last light frames her by the window,
A young woman with distance in her gaze,
She could never imagine the surprise
That is hovering over her life now.

The sentence awakens like a raven,
Fluttering and dark, opening her heart
To nest the voice that first whispered the earth
From dream into wind, stone, sky and ocean.

She offers to mother the shadow's child;
Her untouched life becoming wild inside.

THE VISITATION

In the morning it takes the mind a while
To find the world again, lost after dream
Has taken the heart to the underworld
To play with the shades of lives not chosen.

She awakens a stranger in her own life,
Her breath loud in the room full of listening.
Taken without touch, her flesh feels the grief
Of belonging to what cannot be seen.

Soon she can no longer bear to be alone.
At dusk she takes the road into the hills.
An anxious moon doubles her among the stone.
A door opens, the older one's eyes fill.

Two women locked in a story of birth.
Each mirrors the secret the other heard.

THE NATIVITY

No man reaches where the moon touches a woman.
Even the moon leaves her when she opens
Deeper into the ripple in her womb
That encircles dark to become flesh and bone.

Someone is coming ashore inside her.
A face deciphers itself from water
And she curves around the gathering wave,
Opening to offer the life it craves.

In a corner stall of pilgrim strangers,
She falls and heaves, holding a tide of tears.
A red wire of pain feeds through every vein
Until night unweaves and the child reaches dawn.

Outside each other now, she sees him first.
Flesh of her flesh, her dreamt son safe on earth.

THE PRESENTATION IN THE TEMPLE

The words of a secret have rivet eyes
That cannot sleep to forget what they know.
The restrained voice sharpens to an arrow
That will reach its target through any disguise.

Two old people wait in the temple shadows
Where stone and air are hoarsened with prayer
For some door to open in their hunger;
Sometimes children laugh at her twitching nose.

Worn to a thread the old man's rope of days,
Spent unravelling in this empty torment,
Has wizened his silence to words of flint.
When he glimpses the child, his lost voice flares.

His words lodge in the young mother's thought
That a sword of sorrow will pierce her heart.

THE FINDING IN THE TEMPLE

Oblique to the heart, the word a man seeks
Seldom comes to life in a tongue of flame
From the grate of silence where anger dreams
And stutters in embers thought cannot reach.

When the voice remains fettered, it grows cold
All over the neighbourhood of the word.
In the heart distance cries out to be heard,
When night burns with the face of the beloved.

He is old, yet still betrothed to her dream
That took their home into its possession.
He dwells beside her, anxious and alone.
Hopes when this ends, he will reach her again.

They search the crowd for the child who is gone.
He tells the strangers that it is his son.

THE AGONY IN THE GARDEN

Whatever veil of mercy shrouds the dark
Wound that stops weeping in no one, cannot
Stop the torrent of night when it buries thought
And heart beneath the black tears of the earth.

Through scragged bush the moon discovers his face,
Dazed inside the sound of Gethsemane,
Subsiding under the weight of silence
That entombs the cry of his terrified prayer.

What light could endure the dark he entered?
The void that turns the mind into a ruin
Haunted by the tattered screeching of birds
Who nest deep in hunger that mocks all care.

Still he somehow stands in that nothingness;
Raising the chalice of kindness to bless.

THE SCOURGING AT THE PILLAR

When we love we love to touch the beloved.
Our hands find joy in the surprise of skin.
Here is where tenderness is uncovered.
Few frontiers hold a world more wondrous in.

Imagine the anger of their disturbance.
They cannot bear the portals his words create.
Helpless, turned inside out by his presence,
Sheltering from themselves as a crowd irate.

Made to face the pillar, the wrists bind him
Under the shadow of the angel of pain,
Who flogs, and waits, prefers a broken rhythm,
Until his back becomes a red text of shame.

His mind holds to the images of those he loves;
While his frightened skin swells under the scourge.

THE CROWNING WITH THORNS

The thorns woven to your head are nothing
Like the emptiness loosening your mind
From the terse mountains where you served your time
Seeking the hearth in the loneliness of things.

Then that slow glimpse of three faces concresced
In a circle of infinitely gentle gaze
Trusting each thing out of air into form,
Showed you belong to this first tenderness.

You earth divine flame in a young man's frame.
Things rush your senses offering their essence.
Now the earth clenches against you, cold and closed
In a yard forsaken by every name.

On crucifixion duty, bored with routine
The soldiers start mocking and crown you king.

THE CARRYING OF THE CROSS

A kiss on the back of the neck tingles,
Almost sound, a breath of music in bone.
It is here they laid the heavy crossbeam,
Each step a thud inward like sick thunder.

It invades his head. All silence leaves him.
Stooped forward he watches his innocent feet
Search each step for sure ground to take the weight.
He falls face first on the broken pavement.

Those he knows to see will not meet his eyes.
They fear his gaze might unleash misfortune.
Sweat down his back opens a line of wounds.
A white towel absorbs a mirage of his face.

Windows open in the crowd, his heart rends
At the weeping of his mother and friends.

THE CRUCIFIXION

When at last it comes, it comes in silence;
With no thought for the one to whom it comes,
Or how a heart grieves itself and loved ones
With that last glimpse from its fading presence.

Yet it is intimate, the act of death,
To be so chosen, exposed and taken.
Nowhere untouched. But death wants you broken.
The soldiers must wait ages for your last breath.

With all the bright words, you are found out too,
In agony and terror in vaulted air,
Your mind bleached white by a wind from nowhere
That has waited years for one strike at you.

A slanted rain cuts across the black day.
It turns stones crimson where the cross is laid.

⇥ The Glorious Mysteries ⇤

THE RESURRECTION

Oh, the rush with which the forgotten mind awakens
Under the day a well of dark where colour dwells
Until it learns the art of light and can reveal,
In neglected things, the freshness thought darkens.

With grey mastery distance starts to blur the horror.
Already the days begin to set around the loss.
The after-silence of his death becomes porous
To the gossip of regret that follows failure.

Through the cold, quiet nighttime of the grave
    underground,
The earth concentrated on him with complete longing
Until his sleep could recall the dark from beyond
To enfold memory lost in the requiem of mind.

The moon stirs a wave of brightening in the stone.
He rises clothed in the young colours of dawn.

THE ASCENSION

With waves the ocean soothes the dark stillness of
  the shore.
With words the mind would calm the awful, inner quiet.
Offerings to the nothingness on which we trespass.
Our imprint no deeper than breath on a mirror.

Though delighted by the wonder of your return,
To glimpse you is already too much for their eyes.
At your cadence of voice a bird stirs in the heart,
Its wings spread such brightness nothing can hold its form.

You are no longer from here, yet you still linger
In the lightness, wed to the dance you awaken,
As if in drudged-down lives, the song of your new hands
Could raise the soul towards horizons of desire.

You slip through a door of air. Memory comes home,
Bright as a dead tree drawn to blossom by the moon.

THE DESCENT OF THE HOLY SPIRIT

Somewhere in our clay remembers the speed of cold,
Overtaking the surge of colours with grey breath,
And the shudder of fields, as they smother beneath
The white infinity of ice paralysing the world.

How swiftly fear touches this relic-cold in the bone.
After his second going, they hide from the crowd.
Then, like manna from a red wind, a tongue of
    flame swirls
Into each mind huddled there in the fear-filled room.

The language caul they lived in falls, leaves them wordless,
Then, a kindling, words they never knew they had come
Alive out of nowhere sprung with awakening
That will not cease until winter sets the heart free.

Out in the open now, voices of new belonging,
Needing no courage beyond the fire of their longing.

THE ASSUMPTION

Perhaps time is the keeper of distance and loss,
Knowing that we are but able for a little at a time.
And the innocence of fragments is wise with us,
Keeps us from order that is not native to our dust.

Yet, without warning, a life can suddenly chance
On its hidden rhythm, find a flow it never knew.
Where the heart was blind, subtle worlds rise into view;
Where the mind was forced, crippled thought
    begins to dance.

As if this day found for her everything she lost.
Her breath infused with harvest she never expected
From the unlived lives she had only touched in dream;
Her mind rests; memory glows in a stairs of twilight.

Her hair kisses the breeze. Her eyes know it is time.
She looks as young as the evening the raven came.

THE CORONATION

It was a long time ago in another land.
Who can tell how it really was before belief
Came towards you with a hunger that could not see you
Except against white air cleansed of the shadow of earth?

No inkling that you were a free spirit who loved
The danger of seeing the world with an open mind,
How you strove to be faithful to uncertainty
And let nothing unquestioned settle in your heart.

You loved to throw caution to the wind when you danced.
To be outside in the dawn before people were,
Letting the blue tides of your dreaming settle ashore.
The village said you put the whole thing into his head.

In the glow of your silence, the heart grows tranquil.
No one will ever know where you had to travel.

DISTANCES

The antelope are the only creatures
swift enough to catch the distance.
—LOUISE ERDRICH

Every thought should recall the ruin of a smile.
—E. M. CIORAN

Because the outer walls of God are glass.
—ANNE CARSON

WORDS

For Ethel and Sheila

Words may know the way to reach the dark
Where the wild sweetness of a hillside
Is distilled in a hive under grass.

Words may tell how the rhythm of tide
Can soften its salt-voice on the shore
Through music it steals when stone confides.

Words may capture how the ravens soar
In silk black selves far into the blue
To seek the nest of night's colour hoard.

Words may live under ground out of view
Holding a vanished world etched in scrolls
Under sands where streets lay and youth grew.

When the red vapour breathes through the soul
And pain closes down the ease of the day
Words stagger back to silence and fold.

WINGS

For Josie

Whenever a goose was killed,
My mother got the two wings.
They were placed on the rack
Over the black Stanley range
And taken down to sweep
Around the grate and the floor.

Local women said: no matter
How you sprinkled it, every time
You'd sweep a concrete floor,
You'd get more off it.
As if, deep down,
There was only dust.

Often during sweeping,
A ray of light
Through the window

Would reveal
How empty air
Could hold a wall
Of drunken dust.

Instead of being folded around
Each side of a living body,
Embracing the warmth
And urgency of a beating heart,
The wings are broken objects now,
Rubbed and rubbed, edge down
Into an insatiable floor,
Smothered and thinned,
Until they become ghost feathers
Around a cusp of bone
Polished by motherly hand.

Never again to be disturbed
Every year by the call
Of the wild geese overhead,
Reminding them of the sky,
Urging them to raise the life
They embrace, to climb the breeze
Beyond the farm, towards horizons
That veil the green surge of the ocean.

THE TRANSPARENT BORDER

There is a strange edge to the wind today,
Some irritation with the patient strain
Of trees, the 'willing to bend with anything'
Trick of the rushes, the shoals of shadow
Perplexing the lake and all the silent
Aloofness of the stones, something
Very old, perhaps, resentment towards
These bog fields, each rooted in its dark
Continuum and known to people by name
And season, from which many stones
Have been claimed to make houses
Where they grow warm with human echoes,
And the lake, to which the mountains come
To mirror themselves, where twilights linger
Before night sends everything to rest;
A resentment at the way they all somehow
Slipped across the transparent border

From idea into individual thing,
Glistening with name, colour and form
At the beginning, when the wind would have
Felt breath was where presence lived.

THE ANGEL OF THE BOG

For Lelia

The angel of the bog mourns in the wind
That loiters all over these black meadows.
Remembers how it chose branches to strum
From the orchestra of trees that stood here;
How at twilight a chorus of birds came
To silence in nests of darkening air.

Raindrops filter through leaves, silver the air,
Wash off the film of dust to release nets
Of fragrance on which the wind can sweeten
Before expiring among the debris
That brightens each year with fallen colour
Before the weight of winter seals the ground.

The dark eyes of the angel of the bog
Never open now when dawn comes to dress
The famished grass with splendid veils of red,
Amber, white, as if its soul were urgent
And young with possibility and dreams
That a vanished life might become visible.

PLACENTA

For Máire Bheag

It grew between you
Naturally.
This wise wall
That took everything
From you
He needed.

Grew varicose,
To carry through
The seepage of calcium.
Holding rhythm,
Offering time,
To structure and settle
The white scribble
Until it finds

The stillness
And strength
Of bone.

Fed the beat
Of your pulse
Through the dark,
A first music,
To steady the quiver
That would become
His heart.

Sieved from the stream
Of your breathing,
The breath of trees,
Fragrance of flowers,
The heavy scent of woman,
Chorus of seas,
Ripples of the ancestral,
And the strange taste
Of a shadow-father,
When you kissed.

Feels towards the end
The temper of flow change
And absorbs the white stream
To urge the child free.

On your own,
Now,
Growing away
From each other.
Nothing
Between you
But the distance
That will remain
Alive
With invisible tissue.

MOUNTAIN-LOOKING

For the Burren Action Group
who saved Mullach Mór

The mountain waits for no one
But rises on its own to overlook

The blind spread of fields and
The local pride of trees adept
At the art of singular ascent.

The lakes which stay in place,
Somehow held up by the threaded
Resolve of the bog that rusts the water
Until it takes dark for depth.

The grey certainty of the stones,
Stained yellow with moss and lichen,
Who serve as sentinels among the bushes,

Alert for the whisper of the ice
That will return to retrieve them
In white nests from the loose air.

And the earth-orphans
In their strong homes
That light up at night
On sealed ground
Where they shelter from
The seamless totality of the dark
Claiming all the spaces of separation.

Watched by animals,
They emerge at daytime;
No surface here
Could wear frowns
Like these faces.
Their limbs and eyes
Blurred with desire,
They climb up sometimes
Hoping, maybe,
To see what the summit sees.

SEDUCED?

In the empty carton
Inside the door of the attic,
Five blue crystals wait
To entice the visitors
Who will come in the dark,
Breath seduced
By the distant scent
Of such blue delight.

Frost and hunger
Will bring them in
To the labyrinth
Of breathing spaces
That run through
The stone walls.

They will never see
How beautiful

The walls are on
The other side, the warm
Surfaces of soft peach
That shelter the joy
Of love, music and thought,
With windows toward
Mountains adored by light.

While you sleep,
They will feast
In the dark,
Lick and chew
Each minuscule fibre
Of the forbidden food,
Replace the blue
With emptiness.

By the time
Thirst takes them,
Desperately,
Down to the lake
It will already
Be too late.

AT THE EDGE

Sometimes, behind the lines
Of words giving voice to the blue wind
That blows across the amber fields
Of your years, whispering the hungers
Your dignity conceals, and the caves
Of loss opening along shores forgotten
By the ocean, you almost hear the depth
Of white silence, rising to deny everything.

UP THE MOUNTAIN

Was it a choice once,
From within such trembling,

To make a desperate lunge out of here,
Push the fields up into the air,

And make a summit high
Above neighbouring ground offering itself

To host the annual desire of flowers
Emerging like debutantes amidst grass?

Unwilling to linger further under stones,
Endure aimless animal hunger,

And the anger of the trees
Always departing in two directions.

Today the mountain is clear.
It won't suffer the rain.

The deluge of tears from a sky
Barking in thunder,

But sends the white rivers down
With desperate music

Into the fields of quiet.

PRISONS OF VOICE

Don't ask me to walk here
These mountains come too near
Something distance never healed.

In this light, blue and high,
They pretend to be horizons
Claiming the affections of the eye.

But in their concealed cloister
They hold each voice captive
To tune dead stone with narrative.

THE OCEAN WIND

Through its mouth at Gleann Corráin, the rising
Ocean can see into Fermoyle valley
That never moves from the absence opened
By the cut of its glacier parent.
With wind the ocean bends each lone blackthorn
To a dark sickle facing the mountain.

The wind would like to breathe its crystal breath
Into the mind of the mountain's darkness
And riddle the certainty of its stone;
It lashes the cliffs with doubt, its sand lips
Deepen the question each crevice opens
And sow hoards of fern seed in the scailps.*

There is no satisfaction for the wind.
To blow through doors and windows of ruins
Only reminds it how empty it is.

---

*The clefts in limestone pavement

Above Caherbeanna's ruined village
The wind waits all year for the Garraí Clé
To fill with its tribe of golden corn.

Weary from the ghost geometry of the fog
And heaping itself blindly against walls,
The wind unfolds its heart in yellow dance;
Only now in circles, spirals and waves
Of corn can the wind see itself, swift
As the glance of moonlight on breaking tide.

OUTSIDE A COTTAGE

They allow themselves to be strangers.
Here is somewhere else for them;
They hunt for images to take back
To perfectly ordered cupboards
In Germany or the States,
Proud to have captured
Something authentic of the place.

When the bus drops them,
The cameras come out
To snap the cottage ruin,
Rimmed against the black desert
Of bog and overgrown mountains
With the bones out through them.

They shoot the ruin, not sensing
How the image is a relic,

Imprinted with the presence
Of the ones who laboured here,
The stones warm with breath,
From the time a tourist was a wonder.

Will these ever know how it was,
To live here and know nowhere else,
To wake up inside this house once,
And come out at dawn to discover
Gifts left at the door in the night,
A shivering lake between flowering granite
And this line of new, blue mountains?

BREAKAGE

Has to. Crack. Wet street.
Her first car stops.

•

His children's eyes. Can't meet his.
Old folks' home.

•

Said why. Wrote name with care: Susan.
Then did it.

•

No sleep. The voices own you.
They take you with them.

•

If she knew, she'd go. But she doesn't.
Happy.

DOUBLE EXPOSURE

Sometimes you see us
Run into each other in a place
Where we cannot simply pass,
Say at a party, and you overhear
Our breath quiveringly collect
To shape a voice sure enough
To play out some pleasantry;
Something humorous is preferable,
It covers perfectly and shows
That everything is as it should be.
As smoothly as possible
We allow ourselves to be waylaid
By some other conversation and escape.
Though we move around the room,
We always know where we stand,
Still strangely bound to each other
In this intermittent dance

Between the music, each careful
To hold up the other side of all
We were to each other before
It stopped, and let nothing slip
From the invisible ruin
We carry between us.

ELEMENTAL

Is the word the work
Of some elder who quarries
The green mountain
For the hard deposit,
Refines it under black dust
That a bellows blows red,
Hammers it to a wafer
On the white anvil
Until it can carry its own loss,
The anger of the withering fire,
The unstruck echo of the mountain,
Yet succumb to breath
Like pollen to the breeze?

THE NIGHT

February 1, 1994

Nothing can make the night stay outside,
It pours in everywhere, smothers my room
With black air prepared in some unseen cave,
Tightens around my skull the root silence
Of that room in rock; nothing broke the dark
Except the tick of raindrops from above;
Centuries seeping through the limestone
To point a cold finger of stalactite
At emptiness never softened by breath;
Where the sore of absence was never felt
In cold that fasted solid from light,
A hermit space that let in no question.
This dark is all eyes; but cannot feel
How it blackens the breath and the heart.
It weighs me down as it would a stone.

ANCHOR

For Laurie

Everything
Depends
On the fall
Being utterly
Helpless
A meteor shaft
Of dead weight
Slicing through
Dreaming water
Aiming straight
At weakness
Underneath
In the stone
Destination
To vent

A wound
Desperate enough
To grip and hold
The strain
Of a pilgrim vessel
Swaying in the dark
On a surface
Where storms sleep
Lightly.

A BURREN PRAYER

Oremus,
Maria de Petra Fertilis:

May the praise of rain on stone
Recall the child lost in the heart's catacomb.

May the light that turns the limestone white
Remind us that our solitude is bright.

May the arrival of gentians in their blue surprise
Bring glimpses of delight to our eyes.

May the wells that dream in the stone
Soothe the eternal that sleeps in our bone.

May the contemplative mind of the mountain
Assure us that nothing is lost or forgotten.

May the antiphon of ocean on stone
Guide the waves of loneliness home.

May the spirits who dwell in the ruin of Corcomroe
Lead our hearts to the one who is beautiful to know.

Go maire na mairbh agus a mbrionglóidí
I bhfoscadh chaoin dílis na Trinóide.*

---

*May the departed and their dreams ever dwell
In the kind and faithful shelter of the Trinity.

Page 13 The authoritative work on the Banshee tradition in
Irish folklore is Patricia Lysaght's *The Banshee: The Irish Death
Messenger* (Roberts Rinehart, 1996).

Page 19 This poem takes its title from the title of a photo-
graph by the Conamara photographer Fergus Bourke.

Page 33 The rosary is a form of devotion accompanying the
contemplation of fifteen mysteries highlighted from the life of
Jesus. They are divided into the Joyful, Sorrowful, and
Glorious Mysteries. Fifteen decades of Hail Marys are recited;
each decade is preceded by an Our Father and followed by a
Glory Be to the Father. This devotion is usually prayed on
rosary beads, consisting of a sequence of beads which repre-
sent the five decades corresponding to one set of the myster-
ies. According to the theologian Noel Dermot O'Donoghue,
the rosary enfolds the mystical heart of Christianity. The
name "rosary" comes from the flower, the rose, which in the
medieval period was understood as a symbol of life eternal.
The rosary in its present form emerged in late medieval
Christianity.

Page 34 This poem was first written in Irish, and "The
Rosary" is the English translation.

Page 63 Mullach Mór is a spectacular mountain in the Burren
in the West of Ireland. It has been the subject of a recently
successful ten-year environmental campaign by the Burren
Action Group to prevent the Irish government from building
an interpretation centre for tourists there.

Page 83 Corcomroe is the ruin of a twelfth-century Cistercian
monastery in the Burren. It was dedicated to Maria de Petra
Fertilis: Mary of the Fertile Rock.